For Stephen

A Very Good Middle Shepherd Indeed

THE RELUCTANT SHEPHERD

Monica Withrington

The Reluctant Shepherd

CHAPTER ONE

SPOOKED BY A CHRISTMAS CARD

Tim pushed back his duvet and sat up. At once the icy air wrapped itself around him, but that was good. It must have snowed – he could almost smell it.

Gleefully, he scrambled off the bed and padded to the window. He could picture the snow drifts, a hundred feet high. He wouldn't be able to open the front door – maybe the whole house was buried and the Emergency Services would have to come and dig them all out! He'd prayed for snow last night – really prayed: fallen asleep praying. If there was snow outside, then they'd have to close the school and he wouldn't have to…

But when he pulled back the curtain and peered down Long Close, all he could see was a shiny, wet ribbon of black tarmac under the lamplight. It was frosty, but no way was it snowy. Tim sat back on his heels, all hope draining from him. His prayer hadn't worked. School was going to happen as usual, and as for the Dress Rehearsal – well, that was going to happen, too.

But, just before he let the curtain drop, something flashed at the end of the street. A tall figure in a dark uniform, his big red postbag slung over one shoulder, had just entered the Close and was now zig-zagging from driveway to driveway, stuffing brown and white bundles through the letterboxes. As he passed under each street lamp, the reflectors on his jacket shone gold, just for a moment. Then why, Tim wondered, did the bag seem to be lit up, glowing like Rudolph's nose, and getting brighter all the time?

The postman whistled as he strode up the drive of Number Thirty-five. Any minute now, he would be at Tim's door – Number Thirty-nine, dropping a pile of Christmas cards on to the mat. His disappointment forgotten for the moment, Tim ran out on to the landing and had almost reached the top of the stairs, when a ginger streak sprang from the room opposite. An elbow thumped into his side, knocking him into the wall and making him squeak like a rubber toy.

"Oh, Sophie!" Tim wailed, clutching his chest. She was already ahead of him, leaping down the stairs. She was going to beat him to the front door – and the post – again.

"You two!" their mother shouted from the kitchen. "You're worse than puppy-dogs fighting over a bone!"

By the time Tim had reached the bottom step, Sophie was carrying a fistful of envelopes, dropping some and crumpling others, into the kitchen.

"Sophie, do be careful with those," said her mother, who was slipping slices of wholemeal into the toaster. "And Tim – what do you think you're doing? You're not even dressed!"

"Here's one for me and Tim!" Sophie shouted in triumph. "From Auntie Judy, I bet." Then, her tone changed to one of surprise. "Hey, Tim!" she said, "Here's one for you!"

"So?" Tim retorted. "It's allowed, isn't it?" And he snatched the card from his sister. For a moment, he stared at the snowy envelope. On the outside there was just one word: TIM. No surname and no address. And the stamp looked like nothing he'd ever seen before. Where there should have been the head of the Queen, and a number saying '1st', or '2nd', there was a big star in a midnight blue sky and some strange squiggles, like curled-over walking sticks. Something tickled the palm of his hand, then the envelope slithered on to the floor.

"Butterfingers," Sophie scolded, picking it up. But Tim just stood there. That tickling feeling had not come from him, he was sure: it had come from inside the envelope. He could have sworn he had felt it squirm. Sophie was saying something. "Open it, then – or shall I?"

"No, I will," said Tim, recovering enough to snatch it back.

"Oh, how sweet," simpered Sophie, peering over her little brother's shoulder, as he carefully undid the flap and pulled out a perfectly ordinary Christmas card. "A boy shepherd with a lamb. Who's it from, then? One of your girl friends?"

The words inside were printed in gold letters. "Dear Tim," they said, "I'm sending you this little shepherd boy to help you in the Play. Good Luck." There was no signature.

"So, who's it from?" Sophie repeated.

"Nobody you'd know," said Tim, pulling a face, as he threw the card down on to the kitchen table.

"Now, now," said his mother, "none of that, please."

"But I don't want to be a shepherd," he said. "I don't want to be in the play. It's babyish."

"You're babyish, you mean," trumpeted Sophie. She had landed the most desirable role – that of Angel Gabriel – and it was going to her head: Big Time.

Tim glared at his big sister. Her crown of red-gold hair was perfect for an angel. She hardly needed the tinsel halo her mother had made her. What a pity she wasn't angelic all the way through, not just on the outside, he thought.

"Anyway, you don't have to go on stage with your dressing-gown on back to front and a stupid tea-towel on your head," Tim growled.

"Well, you've got to play a shepherd," said Sophie. "Mrs. Adams says so."

Most of the time, Tim liked his tiny, village school. But being at a small school had its problems, too. There were only nine pupils in Miss Rennie's Reception class, this year – barely enough to act out a Nativity Play. So Mrs. Adams, the headmistress, had insisted that the whole school – sixty pupils in all – should take part.

"For the last time," said his mother, "will you go upstairs and get dressed!"

When Tim came downstairs again, this time in his grey trousers and maroon school sweatshirt, Sophie was just finishing off her toast. "Can't wait for the Dress Rehearsal today," she sang, as soon as he was within earshot.

"Why do we have to have a Dress Rehearsal?" moaned Tim, digging his spoon into his bowl of Coco Pops. It was all right for Sophie: she had a proper costume, not like his.

"Mrs. Adams likes to get things perfect," said Sophie. "She says we'll play our parts better when we look right."

Mrs. Adams can dream on, thought Tim.

"Time you were off," called their mother. "Don't forget your costumes."

"Where?" asked Tim, looking round without seeing anything. "I think I've lost mine."

Sophie was gently swinging a Tesco's carrier bag. "Try the porch," she said. "Mum and I put everything ready there last night, so we wouldn't miss anything."

As he passed the living room on his way to the front door, Tim noticed with some irritation that someone had put his card on the mantelpiece. He stopped to look at the small figure in the centre – carrot-coloured hair sticking out from under the checked head-cloth, button nose – freckles even. Trust the mystery sender to find a card which was almost a clone of himself. The shepherd boy seemed to look Tim straight in the eye.

Then, he winked.

CHAPTER TWO

DRESSING-GOWNS AND TEA-TOWELS

Tim bolted into the porch, snatched up the plastic bag he found lying there and hurtled out of the house, slamming the front door behind him. He pounded down the pavement after his sister, who had already set off down Long Close towards the Village School.

"Try taking the door right off its hinges next time, why don't you?" Sophie said, helpfully.

But she hadn't understood. His Christmas card was spooked! He hadn't been able to get out of the house fast enough!

Halfway along the Close, Sophie said, "Aren't you going to call for Alex?"

"Yeah," Tim lied. "I was just going." He had been so busy thinking about the Christmas card that he had completely forgotten his best friend. Now, he trotted up the drive of Number Seventeen and pressed the bell. 'We wish you a Merry Christmas' chimed electronically on the other side of the door. Alex's doorbell played a different tune for every season.

"Hi!" Tim's friend, beaming all over his chubby face, came spilling out on to the path as he juggled with anorak, trainers, a football, 'Spurs' lunch box and a Sainsbury's carrier bag.

"Hi," said Tim. Why, Tim wondered, was Alex always so cheerful? Being best in the class in Literacy and Maths hardly made him the most popular boy in school; and he was rubbish at football. It must be because he didn't have a sister bugging him every hour of the day.

"Got your dressing-gown there?" Alex asked as they set off down the Close once more. "What colour is it?"

"Blue," Tim mumbled. "What colour is yours?"

Alex had apparently been waiting for the question because his face lit up as he said, "Striped. It's new. I'm getting it for Christmas."

"Then how come you've got it already?"

"Mum's letting me use it for the Play. I chose it 'specially – look." He pulled a small piece of cloth out of the Supermarket bag. It was made of towelling material, woven into fine stripes in maroon, dark green and a sort of coffee colour. It was really rather smart – perfect for the Innkeeper, which was the part Alex had been chosen to play.

"Tim!" a voice squeaked as Tim, Alex and Sophie passed through the school gates and headed towards their classroom door.

"Oh, no," Tim groaned. He half turned towards the pale blue Mercedes parked by the kerb, out of which a tiny boy was scrambling, blond curls bouncing above an angelic face.

"Your fan club wants you," sniggered Sophie, as the infant struggled to catch up with the bigger boys. His knees buckled under the weight of his Lazy Town satchel, which was almost the same size as he was.

"Aren't you going to wait for him?" Alex asked.

"George Wilkie is such a baby," muttered Tim. He was another reason why Tim didn't want to play Middle Shepherd. Ever since George had been cast as the Smallest Shepherd, Tim had found himself in the role of nursemaid, having to look after him, telling him when to go on stage and where to stand. "You don't have to put up with him following you around all day like a little dog," he said to Alex.

"Look what I've got." George drew level at last, pink in the face from the effort. He was holding out something white and fluffy.

"Cool," said Alex. "Is that your lamb? Have you brought it for the play?"

"To give to the Baby Jesus," said George breathily.

"Yeah, right," said Tim, trying unsuccessfully to show some enthusiasm. "That's great. Just what we need for our scene. Mmmm. Nice feet. Black."

As George beamed at his hero, a flock of tiny girls appeared from nowhere and fluttered round him like sparrows, chirruping and cooing, as one by one they fingered the toy lamb. Tim and Alex took their chance and slunk away.

In Year 3 and 4's cloakroom, bulky dressing-gowns bulged out of bags; long white dresses hung from coat hooks and tinsel crowns hung or lay about all over the place. Alex and Tim dumped their supermarket bags as close to their coat hooks as they could manage.

"Have you got a tea towel for your head?" Alex asked Tim.

"I think so," he muttered. "And you?"

"Sure. Stripes or checks?"

"Can't remember," said Tim. "Checks, I think." Well, it was a checked one that he'd used last time he'd helped with the drying up.

"Mine's striped; red, yellow and blue," said Alex. Tim wanted desperately to change the subject. What was this interest in tea-towels, all of a sudden?

"Show us your dressing-gown, then," Alex begged. Tim obediently reached inside his bag and felt for the fluffy material. As he drew it out, his head began to spin. What was happening to him? The object in his hand wasn't Royal blue:

it was white, with a pink satin edging, and covered all over in cute little rabbits, some pink, some blue and some yellow. This was not his – it was Sophie's old dressing-gown – the one she had grown out of. Sophie, he thought. What a mean trick! I'll kill her!

CHAPTER THREE

A BAD START

There came a nasty chuckle from behind him. Tim felt his neck prickle, as a broad figure wedged itself between him and Alex.

"Well, you're sure going to look sweet in that, Shepherd boy," Warren Chesney gloated. There was only one bigger bully in the school than Warren, and that was his older brother, Craig. No one argued with them – no one who wanted to keep his skin on, that was. Warren was the third reason why Tim didn't want to be a shepherd in the play. He had been cast as Big Shepherd, and had assumed that this had given him the right to make Tim's and George's lives as miserable as possible.

Fiercely, Tim fought back his tears. "My funny old sister," he exclaimed, forcing himself to laugh. "She's such a practical joker!" Alex immediately joined in.

"She's got a sense of humour, your sister, that's for sure," he chortled, just as unconvincingly. "Come on, Tim. Let's go in. She'll probably swap the dressing-gowns over while we're not looking, if I know her."

Holding their heads high, the boys pushed open the door to their classroom.

"Hurry up, boys," Mrs. Hodge fussed. "You're making us late. We've got such a lot to get through today – and that's before the Dress Rehearsal."

Tim flung himself on to his chair. This day wasn't going well – not well at all: and it had barely begun! It was the postman's fault. Should he tell Alex about the strange card, he wondered? Would he understand, or label him a basket case, especially after the dressing-gown incident?

Even in December, with Christmas streamers floating above their heads and the Tree with its hand-made decorations filling one corner of the classroom, Mrs. Hodge liked to begin the day with Maths. But first she always chatted to the class and asked them if they had any news.

"There will be a full Dress Rehearsal for the Play after Break," she told her pupils. "I hope you've all got your costumes ready."

Lucy's hand went up. "My Mum asked if there are any spare wings for the Angel Choir. She hasn't made mine yet, 'cos she didn't have the right things."

"That's all right, Lucy," said Mrs. Hodge. "As long as you have a white dress and some tinsel for your hair. Mrs. Adams has lots of angel wings. Are there any more questions about costumes?" Alex glanced across at Tim.

"Tell her," he whispered. Tim shook his head. He could see Warren Chesney watching him. "She'll have a fit when she finds out," Alex went on.

"I'll tell her later – when we're changing," Tim whispered back.

"Or not – as in your case," muttered Alex.

"Anything wrong over there?" came Mrs. Hodge's voice. Tim looked up. Sixteen pairs of eyes were fixed on him.

"Me?" he said, pretending to be surprised. "No. I'm OK, thanks." He stared down at the Maths books on the table in front of him, wishing, for the first time in his life, that he could get started. Then he heard the word 'Christmas card', and his head jerked up.

Abigail was waving a square object in the air. "It's from me Auntie," she announced. "It's flewed all the way from

15

Jamaica." The bad news was – it was a musical one. It sang 'Jingle Bells' when you opened it. While it was being passed round for everyone to try, playing its pesky little tune over and over, Mrs. Hodge asked if anyone else had received an interesting card.

"I've had six so far," said Gemma.

"I've had seven," Becky boasted. Tim kept his eyes on the cover of his Maths book, and wondered what the class and Mrs. Hodge would say if he announced that he had a card which could wink.

It was a relief, for once, to be doing sums. Tim hoped to blot out the memories of that morning. He would rather have Warren Chesney and his brother, not to mention Sophie, picking on him all day. Thinking about them was nothing compared to the sickly, fluttery feeling which came into his stomach when he thought about the winking Christmas card.

"Timothy–" Mrs. Hodge's voice broke into his thoughts. "What's this on your page?" Mrs. Hodge was very tall and built a bit like a Town Hall; she also had an uncanny way of turning up next to you when you didn't want her to. Now she was towering over him. Tim looked down. The squared paper was adorned with numbers, but none of them looked quite right. The threes and fives were back to front and the fours were upside-down.

"This isn't like you," his teacher remarked. "What's got into you today?"

Tim stared at the page. He could think of nothing suitable to say.

"Do you want to lose your break, young man? I want to see at least ten sums, properly written down, before I let you go."

Tim had an idea. "I could do them during the play practice," he said brightly.

"That would never do," boomed Mrs. Hodge. "Mrs Adams wouldn't allow it. Now here's a rubber. I want all this mess rubbed out. And do try to concentrate this time."

Tim glanced at Alex, hoping to see his friend's reassuring grin. But, instead, to his horror, Alex gave him the most enormous wink. Tim shrank back. He felt dizzy – again.

"Miss, Miss!" came a girl's voice from somewhere. "Tim's going to be sick!"

CHAPTER FOUR

TEMPORARY REPRIEVE

"Here, take a sip." Mrs. Chandler, the School Secretary, offered Tim a tea-cup half filled with cold water. Tim was sitting back in a big arm chair in her office. The room was warm and friendly. There were Christmas cards on her desk beside her computer. None of them looked the sort that might wink. He hadn't been sick; in fact, he didn't even feel sick, much as he wished he could. That would have meant definitely no Dress Rehearsal for him – and possibly no School Play either. Thanking her, he took the cup.

"Can my Mum take me home?" he asked shyly.

"I'm afraid your Mummy isn't home at present," Mrs. Chandler said kindly. "I phoned, but there's no reply. Maybe, if you just sit here for a while, you'll begin to feel better anyway."

Tim was feeling better already. He wasn't much of an actor, and had never fooled his mother into believing he was sick when he wasn't. By the time the classrooms began to empty for break, he was feeling quite hungry, too, and the memory of the Prawn Cocktail flavoured crisps in his lunch box was too much for him. Mrs. Chandler eventually let him go, with the words: "A little fresh air might do you good. Just sit quietly, though – no running about."

"How do you stop a nine-year-old boy from running about?" she asked herself, as Tim shot out of her office.

CHAPTER FIVE

WHO'S AFRAID OF THE THREE WISE MEN?

Despite the wind which whipped across the tarred area of the playground, Tim really didn't feel like running about. He sat on a bench, sheltered by his classroom wall, slowly feeding crisps into his mouth. When Alex caught sight of him, he left the football game he had been taking part in and trotted over to join him.

Tim offered him a crisp. "Thanks," said Alex. "Aren't you sick any more?"

"No, I'm OK, really," said Tim.

"So, what made you fall over like that?"

Tim turned to look straight at his friend. "I'll tell him," he thought. "I'll tell him everything."

"Alex," he began, "why did you wink at me?"

"Why not?" said Alex.

"You've never done it before."

"Yeah," beamed his friend. "I've been practising. I didn't mean to scare you – if that's what did it–"

"No–" Tim began. "It wasn't you that scared me – it wasn't a bad wink, not bad at all."

Alex grinned a wide grin. Tim tried to think how to go on. But suddenly there was a shadow looming above him and something small but very hard was pressing into his foot.

"Oww!" he wailed. "Get off me!" he shouted, as he recognised the huge form of Craig Chesney towering over him. Craig was only ten and a half, but already wore size 8 trainers. Today, he was sporting a pair of new football boots, which, Tim had just painfully learned, had metal studs.

The giant released Tim's bruised foot. Backing him up were his two stooges, Lewis Blaney and Christian Humphries. Being the biggest boys in the school, all three had been cast to play the Three Kings. "It's a wonder Craig wasn't cast as King Herod," Sophie had said a few days before. "He's rubbish at acting. Playing a bully is all he understands." In fact, Herod the Great was to be played by Vishnan Patel, whose dark, Indian good looks seemed to lend themselves to a royal part.

"So – it's Baby Bunnikins, now, is it?" sneered Craig.

"Your baby brother been telling tales again?" asked Alex. "It was a joke, as we explained to him – but he's too dim to understand practical jokes."

"You're insulting my family. I don't like that," snarled Craig, clenching one fist.

"And you're sounding like a gangster movie," Alex responded, shrinking back and covering his face as Craig's heavies moved in.

"Craig Chesney, leave my brother alone!" came a shrill girl's voice from across the playground. "Miss! MISS! Get Craig off my brother!"

The Three Kings backed off as Mrs. Hodge thundered across the playground.

"Listen, you hear!" Craig just had time to say, before he and his heavies skulked away, "You ain't goin' to ruin the School Play by wearing no silly bunny-rabbit costume!"

As his sister stood before him, hands on hips, Tim wondered if the day could get any worse. It was good that she had rescued him from Craig's gang, but there would be a price to pay when they got home.

"So… what was he on about, then?" she demanded.

"Who?" Tim was feeling dizzy again.

"You heard. Craig. He was shouting about bunny rabbits."

"Don't you know?" asked Tim sullenly. "My blue dressing-gown? Somebody's weird sister swapped it for her old one – the bunny one."

"Well, don't look at me," said Sophie. "This play's important to me. Would I ruin it by playing a kid's trick on you like that?"

"How do I know? Nothing's ever stopped you before."

Before any more insults could be exchanged, the whistle announcing the end of Break shrilled across the playground and everyone trotted, raced or pranced back towards the classrooms.

Room Two had already ceased to look like a classroom by the time Tim and Alex entered it. The girls had shed every stitch of school uniform, which now sprawled across the tables and chairs and spilled on to the floor. Mrs. Hodge was bustling about, helping her young pupils as they tugged long white dresses over their heads. David, who was to play the part of Joseph, was down to his Manchester United boxer shorts and was struggling to pull a brown dressing-gown on back to front.

Now Alex held up his early Christmas present for everyone to admire.

"That's gorgeous," said some of the girls.

"He'll look better than Joseph," commented Lucy.

"Quite right," said Mrs. Hodge. "The Innkeeper was probably quite well-off. Joseph was a poor carpenter, remember. Got your costume, I see, Tim," she added, eyeing the supermarket bag in Tim's hand. "Come one, then. We want everyone dressed before the rehearsal begins. Let's see what you've brought."

CHAPTER SIX

DRESS REHEARSAL

"Stupid calling it a dressing-room," thought Tim, as he helped Alex into his new, towelling bathrobe, back to front, of course, and tied the belt behind him. "More of an un-dressing-room." He had no costume to wear, and was to play Middle Shepherd in his school clothes. Mrs. Chandler had finally reached his mother on the telephone. The news wasn't good.

"Your Mum says it's all her fault. As an afterthought, she put some things in another Tesco bag to take to Oxfam. And that's where your dressing-gown is now, I'm afraid. The bags got mixed up. She'll be going back this afternoon to try to rescue it."

Tim had shrugged and pretended not to mind. "I can't be a shepherd, now, can I?" he'd said hopefully.

"Nonsense," Mrs. Hodge had boomed from the other side of the room. "Something will be sorted out by tomorrow."

"Can you help me with my tea-towel?" Alex was asking him. Tim reached up and tried to arrange the piece of striped material on his friend's set of dark, springy curls. It lay there, spread out like a doll's table-cloth. Alex's nose and eyes had disappeared under it.

"There's a tie thing in my bag, said his mouth, and Tim searched until he found a twist of wool, like a sort of rope.

"This it?" he asked, as Alex pushed the cloth back so that his face reappeared.

"It's got to go round my head, somehow," said Alex, "and hold the cloth on."

Mrs. Hodge came to the rescue once more, and soon Alex was looking the very picture of a plump, Bethlehem Innkeeper. Proudly, she surveyed her class. They were transformed. Three wholly believable figures in Biblical dress (Warren, David and Alex) and a choir of angels complete with tinsel halos and coat-hanger wings.

And Tim.

Mrs. Hodge opened the classroom door and one by one her charges filed out into the Hall.

With precision, Mrs. Adams directed each pupil into his or her right place for the opening music. The Angel Choir was seated in two rows on benches along the front. Their tinsel halos were level with the stage and gave it a sparkly fringe.

On one side of the stage stood a pair of clothes-horses hidden by the two large sheets which had been draped over them. Some paper windows had been fixed on to the sheets with safety-pins and a piece of sacking hung down the middle to represent a door. A thick twist of wool had been attached to a small bell and pinned alongside the 'door'.

As the notes of 'Away in a Manger' filtered softly across the stage, the hessian door of this sheet-cottage was pushed aside, and The Virgin Mary, alias Sima, Vishnan's sister, appeared, holding a broom, with which she began sweeping the stage. Sophie, looking every inch an archangel, swooped up the aisle, mounted the stage, and proclaimed to the young girl that she had been chosen to be the Mother of the Son of God; the angel choir stood, sang a carol about Gabriel's Message in soft, breathy voices and sat down again.

The scene now moved to the Royal Palace in Jerusalem. Two scene shifters in angel costumes came on to the stage, struggling with a heavy folding screen, with which they concealed the "cottage". They then produced a chair, painted gold, on which Vishnan, waddling on to the stage, seated himself. As King Herod, he was resplendent in a majestic golden robe, and padded out to make him look enormously fat. His four courtiers now took up their positions, two on either side.

High above the players, an enormous cardboard star, wrapped in tin foil and outlined in tinsel, began to jerk its way on a pulley across the backdrop. When it reached the middle, it stopped, swaying gently. Herod, meanwhile, scanned the horizon, which meant shading his eyes and peering towards the back of the hall. This was the cue for the Three Wise Men to begin processing up the central aisle. Not even the gold paper crowns adorning their heads, or their cloaks of shimmering red, green and blue curtain material were able to disguise the playground thugs that they were. Tim held his breath, waiting for something to go wrong, but, surprisingly, they all played their parts perfectly.

"We seek the One they call the King of Kings," Craig began.

"We have seen His Star in the East, and have come to worship Him," said Lewis, as though he meant every word.

"See, we have brought Him gifts of gold, frankincense and myrrh," said Christian, apparently living up to his name for the first time in his life. Cast and teachers sighed with relief. The worst of their fears were over.

The kings having been sent on their way by Herod, the screen disappeared and now the 'cottage' bore a label which said INN. The angelic scene shifters carried on a large banner bearing the word BETHLEHEM. Now Joseph and Mary appeared on one side of the stage, climbed down the steps there and set out on their 'journey', which meant circling the

Hall once and processing up the centre aisle and back on to the stage. Pulling the bell which had been attached to the sheeting beside the hessian door, they begged Alex to give them a place to sleep, but were turned away and were forced to take shelter among the animals, played by Miss Rennie's Reception class, in tights, tee-shirts and headgear sporting a variety of ears – tall and grey for a donkey, round and mottled brown for a cow and black for sheep.

The two scene-shifters ran on to set up the manger, centre-stage. One carried a stand with cross-over legs, while the other set the crib, filled with hay, on top. It was a flimsy affair, and needed steadying once or twice before the two little angels fluttered off the stage. Then, with the choir singing "Away in a Manger," Mary produced from somewhere under her pale blue cloak a baby doll, which she gently laid in the wobbly crib. The doll's name was Jessica, lent, with great pride, by her 'mother', Emma, in Year 2.

Now, at last, it was the turn of the Shepherds. The choir sang "The First Nowell," as Warren, Tim and little George mounted the 'hillside' towards the back of the stage. This consisted of a tier of benches which had been covered over in brown and green blankets. The trio had barely seated themselves before Sophie swept down the aisle once more and proclaimed "Fear Not! For, behold! I bring you glad tidings of Great Joy!" They immediately jumped up and tried to look fearful. At last, when Angel Gabriel had imparted 'his' message about the birth of the Saviour of the World, the three shepherds – or two shepherds and one school-boy – circled the hall much as Mary and Joseph had done, finally approaching the stage up the aisle. They came to the Inn, where Warren pulled the bell cord so hard that the sheet wall of the Inn fell down, revealing a rather surprised Alex standing between the two clothes horses.

"Behold," shouted Warren, forgot the rest of his line and dissolved into giggles. So did the rest of the cast and the Angel Choir. Teachers rushed to restore the stage, and Warren began again.

"Behold," he bellowed. Again he stopped. Again everyone laughed.

"The Angel," prompted Mrs. Adams.

"The Angel," repeated Warren.

"Of the Lord," said Mrs. Adams.

Bit by bit, Warren struggled through his line, which should have sounded like this: 'Behold, the Angel of the Lord has told us this night that the Messiah has been born in a stable.'

"We wish to see Him," Tim managed to grunt.

"Louder," said Mrs. Adams. "Speak more clearly, Tim."

"WE WISH TO SEE HIM!" bellowed Tim.

"I'M NOT DEAF!" Alex shouted back, covering his ears.

Now, it was George's turn. "Thee, we have bwought him a lickle lamb," he lisped, holding out the fluffy toy. As the innkeeper began to lead the shepherds towards the Manger scene, Warren suddenly snatched the lamb from George, muttering, "I'm the biggest. I should be giving Baby Jesus the lamb."

George stopped, swung round to face the empty hall, stuffed all his fingers into his mouth and howled. Anger boiled up in Tim. He lunged for the lamb, tripped over one leg of the manger and went sprawling on to the stage. The flimsy legs folded and the whole manger collapsed, dumping its pile of hay on top of him. Jessica, meanwhile, rolled out and flopped on to the head on one of the Angels in the choir, knocking her halo sideways, so that it hung over one eye.

Tim lay face-down under the straw and the up-turned

crib and wished that he could be a million miles away –
America, perhaps, or the Planet Mars.

CHAPTER SEVEN

NATHAN

"It doesn't seem to have any batteries," said Alex, turning the Christmas card over in his hand.

He had been quite amazingly understanding when Tim had finally told him about the winking shepherd. "I thought it might be like Abigail's musical one – except with some sort of flashing light instead."

"So, what do you think made it wink?" asked Tim, anxiously. It was, after all, only a piece of stiff paper with a rather good drawing on it.

"When I see things that aren't really there," said Alex, "my dad calls it a trick of the light. Like when a car's headlights shine into the room for a moment or something."

"But I don't remember a car passing," said Tim. When you lived at the top end of a close, very few cars passed your front door.

"This shepherd looks quite harmless to me," said Alex. "Maybe you blinked, and only thought the card was winking."

"Tea's ready," called Tim's mother, and the mystery of the winking shepherd boy was left unsolved for the time being. As the family tucked into sausages and chips, Tim's Mum asked, "So, how was the rehearsal today?"

"OK," said the boys together.

"Tim messed up as usual," said Sophie, licking honey from the edge of a piece of bread.

"It wasn't my fault," said Tim, sulkily.

"You didn't have to wreck the stage," said Sophie. "And you haven't a clue how to speak your lines."

Tim didn't want to cry in front of his friend. Sophie was being downright mean – as usual.

"I didn't feel right – I'm not a shepherd – I never will be one!" The tears started to roll.

"Sophie, you're being unfair," said his mother. To Tim she said, "You'll be fine tomorrow – now that I've got your dressing-gown back. Once you're dressed like a shepherd, you'll feel like one."

"That's right," said Alex kindly. "It feels completely different once you're dressed for the part."

*

That night, just as Tim was climbing into bed, Sophie burst into the room and dumped the mystery card on his bedside table.

"Get some inspiration from that," she sniggered. "You need some after today's mess."

"And you played Angel Gabriel as though you were both the Ugly Sisters at once!" retorted Tim. This was not true, of course. Sophie was a natural – as she knew only too well herself.

For a few moments, Tim stared at the shepherd boy. Only a piece of paper, he repeated to himself. The boy in the picture stared steadily back at him. Both eyes remained wide open. Suddenly Tim felt exhausted. As he turned off his bedside light and sank into slumber, it crossed his mind that there was something not quite right about that shepherd boy.

The feeling that a sack of potatoes had just landed on his feet woke Tim from a pleasant sleep. At the same time, the room was filled with a smell which could only be called at its most polite, farmyard. His eyes flew open, and he saw, in the moonlight, the outline of a figure about his own size, squatting on the end of the bed.

"G–get off me!" he tried to shout, but no sound came out. He fought his duvet in his panic to flee the room.

"It's OK," came a boy's voice. "You know me."

"I do?" queried Tim, finding his voice at last.

"I'm Nathan."

"You are?"

"You know – the shepherd boy."

"S–sorry… I don't know any shepherd boys, not even ones called Nathan," Tim stammered.

"But you know me – I winked at you this morning."

Tim's head began to spin once more. He reached out a shaking hand and switched on his bedside light. One glance was all he needed: the card stood where Sophie had put it; there were the stars, the little town twinkling in the background, the hill on which a few lambs stood or lay – and nothing else. The boy, who should have been tending his flock, was sitting on the end of Tim's bed instead, watching him with bright, amused eyes.

"But how–"

"Did I get here?" Nathan finished the question. "Now that's interesting." The boy waggled a finger thoughtfully. "I went up this hill, above my father's cottage, and when I reached the top, I came to these two tall rocks. When I stood between them – well, I couldn't believe it. I seemed to be staring into a room of some kind."

"This one?" asked Tim.

"No – another one."

"Weren't you scared? I'd have run a mile."

"That was the trouble," said Nathan. "I couldn't run. I was sort of stuck. The rooms kept changing and sometimes it

30

was all dark. I was turned on my head, spun round – it was like being in a nightmare like when you want to run but you can't move. Finally I saw you sort of glaring at me."

"Yes – sorry about that," Tim began.

"It doesn't matter," said Nathan. "I understood what was going on. She's a tough one, your sister. I've got my own name for her – the She-wolf."

Tim giggled. He was beginning to like his new friend.

"Do you still think you're dreaming?" Tim asked. He was having a dream – there was no doubt about that.

"I hope not," said Nathan. "I like this room – that lamp – is it magic?"

"No," said Tim, "just electric. So… if you were stuck on that card over there, how come you're in my room now – and what have you done with your tea-towel?" This was what was wrong with this particular shepherd boy. He could see all his hair, which was sticking up in all directions.

"My what?" inquired the shepherd.

"That cloth thing shepherds wear in Bible pictures."

My cloth-thing, as you call it, is why I'm sitting on your bed-thing," said Nathan cheerfully.

"Sorry, I'm not with you–"

"I was staring at you, sleeping just like my little pet lamb, when a gust of wind came along and blew it off my head. That's when I found I could move again. I tried to catch it, then had to run after it – and here I am. And here it is." He held up a large blue and white checked cloth with a fringe all round it, tied in tassels.

"Where do you live? No, don't tell me – Bethlehem." Tim meant to sound sarcastic.

"How did you guess? Well, we don't actually live in the town, you understand. We have a cottage on the hillside. We spend a lot of the time outside on the hills, of course. Lovely it is on a summer's night, with the stars bright above. It's a bit cold this time of year – we're in winter quarters now."

"Do shepherd boys still wear those sorts of clothes where you come from?" asked Tim, pointing to the long, roughly woven tunic, a bit like a nightshirt, which the boy was wearing.

"Why do you say 'still wear'?" said Nathan.

"Well, it's like…" began Tim. "In the olden days, when Jesus was born, all the men and the boys dressed in – well, like – dressing-gowns back to front. Do they still dress like that?"

"Dressing-gowns? Back-to-front? What are you talking about? And what are you saying about the olden days, when Jesus was born? He was born last autumn."

"Pull the other one," Tim said. "My teacher says He was born hundreds of years ago – two thousand years ago in fact."

"'Pull the other one?' What funny words you use! I can't understand you. What 'other one' must I pull?"

"I don't really know. It's what my Dad says when he thinks I'm not telling him the truth."

"Well, I am telling the truth," said Nathan fiercely. "The Messiah was born in the autumn – I know!" He was almost shouting, now.

"Shh!" said Tim. "You'll wake my Mum and Dad. But – you weren't there, were you? You couldn't have been." Mind you, when a boy wearing something you'd only ever seen in Bible pictures wakes you up at midnight, saying things like he'd just climbed off a Christmas card, you can begin to believe almost anything.

Nathan shook his head sadly. "No… actually, I wasn't. But my father and my brother Benjamin were there – and all the other shepherds on the hill that night when the Angel appeared to them."

"Where were you, then?"

"I was sick – dying, actually." Nathan rose on to his hands and knees, like a dog, and became very excited. "I had the fever. No one had ever recovered from it before. I was really, really, really sick," he said with enthusiasm. "I couldn't move, I was so sick. My neck ached, my muscles ached – all of me was just one big ache!"

"So, what happened?" asked Tim.

"The Messiah – the Baby Jesus – made me better," said Nathan, suddenly solemn.

"You believe that?" asked Tim.

"Sure," said Nathan. "I told you, my Dad and my brother went to see Him. He was born in a cave, where the Innkeeper kept his horses and donkeys – did you know that? My Dad wasn't much of a praying man – not then – but his heart was breaking because he thought I was going to die, so he took a blanket made from our own sheep's wool, and told Benjamin to bring a new-born lamb, and he gave these things as presents to the new Messiah. Then he prayed for me."

"And did you get better straight away?" asked Tim.

"One minute I was lying on my bed down on the floor – burning hot and feeling icy cold at the same time and the next I was sitting up feeling really hungry and asking my Mother for honey cakes. It was that quick."

"That sounds like a real miracle," said Tim, his eyes shining. "Almost as good as going to see the Baby Jesus."

"True," said Nathan, "but I'd have liked to have seen Him just the same."

Suddenly Tim had a most daring idea. "Nathan," he began, "You say you never saw the Baby Jesus – the Messiah." Nathan shook his head. "How would you like to see what happened – not the real thing, you understand – just something like it?"

Nathan looked at Tim suspiciously. "I'm not sure ….."

"It probably won't work – but it might." Tim then went on to explain to Nathan how the story of the Christ Child's birth was still being acted out, all these centuries later, in a special kind of play, called a Nativity Play. "So," he finished, "you're a real shepherd, right? I'm only pretending to be one. We look so alike – when I look at you, I think I'm seeing into a mirror. We could swap places – you could come to my school and pretend to be me, and then you could see what it was like visiting the stable where the Baby Jesus was and all that."

"Ye–e–e–s," said Nathan looking thoughtful, "but…"

"But what?"

"If I take your place, you won't be in the play. Wouldn't that make you sad?"

"Not a bit," said Tim, then, realising he was sounding just a little bit over-enthusiastic, he added, "I can be in the play every year. Giving up my place just this once won't upset me *too* much."

"Well, it would be interesting to see what happens at your school. I've never been to school."

"What, never?"

"I'm a shepherd. I herd sheep. They don't teach you how to bring a new-born lamb into the world, or how to scare wolves away in schools."

"Have you ever scared a wolf?" asked Tim, impressed.

"A few times," said the shepherd boy, with a shrug, as though this was quite normal.

"How old were you when you first had to scare a wolf?" Tim asked.

"I must have been six when I did it on my own. I'd been helping my father for about two years then."

34

"Really? What did you do?"

"Well," said Nathan, "we were all sitting on the hillside overlooking the town. It was a beautiful moonlit night. I had my little pipe, which I had made from a hollow reed, and was playing a tune I had made up myself. Benjamin, my brother, was a bit rude about it and told me to go somewhere else if I wanted to make such a hideous noise. So I wandered down to the nearest stream and up the other side. A few of the sheep had strayed into the valley beyond, I realised, when I got there. I went down to drive them back, when I heard this terrible howl. It chilled my bones. The scariest thing was that it came from my side of the river. Then I saw this shape against the sky. A huge black shadow – wolf-shaped. And I was cut off from the other shepherds by this wailing monster!"

"What did you do?" asked Tim, his heart racing.

"I remembered what Benjamin had said about my pipe-playing," said Nathan. "I started making a sort of howling sound on my pipe, as near as I could get to the noise the wolf made. Sometimes, I wonder if I wasn't saying something insulting in wolf-language with my pipe without knowing it. Anyway, this huge hairy thing suddenly leaped up on its hind legs and went tearing off into the night, as though a thousand demons were after it! I rounded up the sheep and we made our way back to join the rest of the flock."

"That's quite a story," said Tim. "And I suppose you scare them off almost every night, do you?"

"Not every night, no," said Nathan, "but there's always the danger they'll come again – you know. So, are you going to tell your Mother and Father about me?" he asked. "I can't exactly hide."

"Oh, but you can," said Tim. "You could get back on to the card."

"You think so?" asked Nathan. "It may not work."

"If it doesn't work, then you're stuck in this century for ever, and you'll never herd sheep again and never see your parents again, and have to go to school," said Tim.

"Right, you've convinced me," said Nathan, and he crawled on all fours towards the bedside table. As he did so, an amazing thing happened. The closer he got to the card the smaller he seemed to be, until he was barely two centimetres high. He stood up, stepped towards the card as if he were approaching an open door, turned round and waved cheerily at Tim. Then he seemed to freeze there.

Tim stared at his new friend. He hoped that he was all right. Even more, he hoped that he would be able to repeat the trick and take his place in the Nativity Play. It would be a cool thing all round. Suddenly he felt a shiver go through him. He snuggled back under the duvet. His eyes drooped and he gave himself up to a contented sleep.

CHAPTER EIGHT

HEAVENLY BODIES

"This is it, Tim." A distant voice, coming ever nearer: his mother's voice. "Wake up, lazybones," it said softly in his ear. "Play Day. Get up!" A hand was gently shaking him.

Tim turned on to his back, rubbed his eyes and sat up. No light filtered through the curtains. The moon had gone: it was morning, but the winter sun still had a few hours in bed, he guessed. That was more than he could say for himself. He leaned on one elbow and stole a glance toward the card on his bedside-table. Nathan was still on his hilltop, still grinning. Tim blinked. Something had changed. His new friend was proudly wearing his head-cloth once more. So, the events of the night were not part of a weird dream. He really had had a visit from a shepherd boy from Bethlehem.

He leaped out of bed and threw on his school clothes. Down the stairs he ran, taking the last two on his bottom.

"Well," said Sophie over her Frosties, "I never thought I'd see this – my baby brother down to breakfast before eight-thirty!"

"Might as well put on a brave face, eh?" said Tim's Dad, looking over his morning paper. "At least it will all be over by this time tomorrow."

"You're right, Dad," said Tim, trying to sound grown-up. "Exactly what I was thinking myself."

"Little creep," muttered Sophie under her breath. Something wasn't right, and she knew it.

"Check your bag yourself this time, Tim," said his

mother. "Make quite sure you've got your dressing-gown and tea-towel." Tim obligingly pulled out the contents of the supermarket bag his mother was holding out to him.

"It's all there," he said cheerfully. Not that I'm going to need it, he thought. When he went upstairs to brush his teeth, he made sure that he had the most important item with him – the Christmas card.

No one felt much like doing any work at school that day. The play was due to begin at two o'clock, after an early lunch. So there was still the morning to get through. Mrs. Hodge started her pupils on their sums as usual, but there were constant interruptions. A girl or boy from Year 6 kept popping in with a message from Mrs. Adams: could Joseph go through his lines with Mary once more? Now she wanted to rehearse the Innkeeper and the Three Wise Men – could Alex please go into the Hall? Next, Tim and Warren were sent for to practice going through their part without either destroying the scenery or falling over any of the props. When the message came for the whole of the Angel Choir to 'run through' their carols, Mrs. Hodge finally gave up trying to teach anybody anything. Whoever happened to be in her room at any one time was asked to design a Christmas card, instead.

During this quiet time, Tim dared to ask Mrs. Hodge a question.

"Mrs. Hodge," he said, "I've got a friend who says Jesus wasn't born on Christmas Day. He says He was born in the autumn."

"Your friend could well be right," said Mrs Hodge. "No one really knows."

"Then why do we celebrate Christmas on the 25th of December?" Tim asked.

"Well, it goes back to early Christian times," said Mrs.

Hodge. "The Ancient Romans used to celebrate a festival called the Saturnalia, in honour of one of their gods, Saturn."

"Like the planet," put in David, who was busily drawing a Christmas card with a rocket hurtling towards earth.

"Quite right, David," said Mrs. Hodge. "This festival was very popular in Rome, because it involved parties, the giving of presents, too much eating and drinking, just like the way we celebrate Christmas today, unfortunately. The early Christians, who weren't allowed to worship the Roman gods any more, realised that they were missing out on all the fun, so, since no one knew when Jesus was born, they decided to invent a date for His birth – which just happened to be the same one as the Saturnalia!"

"That's cheating," laughed Alex, who had been listening in.

"At least they got to go to some parties," said Tim. "So, why do we now think it was autumn when Jesus was born?"

"I know that one," said David, who loved anything to do with the stars, and wanted to be an astronomer or a rocket scientist when he grew up. "My Star Book says that two planets came together at the end of September round about the year we think Jesus was born: Mars and Jupiter. They stopped inside the constellation of Pisces and made one huge bright light. That could have been the Star of Bethlehem."

"You are keeping up with your reading, David," said Mrs Hodge. "Also, it's actually very cold in the Holy Land in December – the shepherds wouldn't have been out on the hills when the Angels came in the winter, the way the Christmas carol tells it."

Tim made sure he had the card with Nathan's picture on it when he went into the hall to rehearse his part. He slipped it into his shirt pocket so that the shepherd boy's eyes were just visible. "Now watch carefully," he whispered. In reply, something squirmed against his chest, as though he had a mouse there.

This time, George was allowed to present his toy lamb to the Baby Jesus himself. Mrs. Adams was keeping a firm hand on Warren, while making sure that Tim was between the other two throughout the rehearsal. As they were sent back to their classrooms, Tim asked if he could be excused. Once he was in the cloakroom, he found suddenly that he was not alone.

"It gets really stuffy in your pocket," said a full-sized Nathan beside him.

"So, do you think you'd like to take my place?" Tim asked.

"Suppose so – that's what I'm here for, I guess."

"You don't sound all that keen," said Tim, his heart sinking.

"Well, I'm beginning to see why you don't want to play the part," said Nathan. "You haven't been all that honest with me, have you?"

"What do you mean?" asked Tim, alarmed.

"You're really scared of that big boy, for a start." Nathan had said this quite kindly. "I could feel your heart beating really fast when he came into the hall. And the little one gets on your nerves, would you say?"

"I wish he wouldn't behave so like a baby," Tim moaned.

"That's because he *is* a baby," said Nathan.

"That's a bit rich coming from you," commented Tim. "I thought you were herding sheep when you were four."

"That's because I'm poor," said Nathan. "George hasn't had to go to work like I did. He can be a baby for longer."

"You will play the Middle Shepherd for me, though, won't you?"

"I'll try, but don't blame me if something goes wrong."

"Cool!" squealed Tim, patting his new friend on the back. "Go for it!"

"You and your funny words," muttered Nathan.

CHAPTER NINE

GEORGE'S HERO

The bell for Break rang at last, and all the children sped
noisily into the playground. It was a relief to be outside in the
frosty sunshine, to run and jump and clamber on to the
Assault Course, after the hours in the over-heated school
building. Tim and Alex looked about warily for Craig, but
both he and Warren seemed to have disappeared.

"Let's practice goal kicks," said Alex. It was a mystery to
Tim that Alex was always so eager to try things he was never
going to be any good at. He had never managed to get a goal
past Tim, nor had he ever managed to save one kicked by
him, but still he persisted.

"OK," said Tim and the two boys removed their maroon
sweatshirts, which they placed on the ground to mark out the
goal mouth. With Tim as goal-keeper, Alex charged at the
ball, giving it a vigorous kick. It missed the goal by about a
mile, looping over towards the scrawny little hedge that
marked off the Nature Area. No one was allowed there
without a teacher, because of the pond, so Tim took off after
it at once. The ball landed a foot or so short of the hedge,
and just as Tim was about to pick it up, he heard a sound
coming from the other side. Someone was in the Nature Area
– and that someone was crying.

Cautiously, Tim peered between the scraggy branches of
the hedge. There was George, sobbing helplessly, with Craig
and Warren towering above him, on either side. They were
throwing something back and forth to each other, at the

same time calling out to George.

"Come on, Georgie," they were calling. "Catch it!"

Tim didn't have to take a second look to see what it was they were throwing to one another. It was looking a lot less white and pristine; its limbs were dangling and misshapen.

George, his face glistening with tears and snot, could do nothing as his beloved lamb flew back and forth high above his head.

Tim watched in horror, wondering what he could do. He preferred not to have his feet bruised by Craig's football boot again, or have his face punched in, either. The most sensible thing would be to wait for the brothers to grow bored with their game and then he could take George to Mrs. Chandler to have his face wiped. Suddenly, something kicked him in the breastbone so sharply that he gasped. The next minute, a full-sized Nathan was squeezing through the hedge and putting himself between the Chesney brothers.

"All right," he squeaked at the two huge boys. "So you've had your fun. Now give it back!"

Craig, holding the lamb above his head, paused and stared down at this apparent madman below him. "Well, if it isn't Bunnikins again," he snarled. "Want my boot on the other foot, do you?"

"Wow!" breathed a voice beside Tim. "Do you see that? It's your shepherd – the one on the Christmas card!" Tim hadn't filled Alex in on the latest developments, but it was no longer necessary. Alex was grinning wickedly. "Craig thinks it's you out there!"

"I know," replied Tim. It might not be all good news, either, he was thinking.

"Just give it back!" commanded the shepherd boy.

"Who says?" said Warren.

Nathan changed tactic. "Come on, George," he said,

43

putting an arm round the infant's shoulder, "let's leave these two to their kiddies' game. Who wants to watch two big babies playing catch with a fluffy toy, anyway? It's really boring." He started leading George away, at the same time whispering something in his ear.

The two brothers stopped and stared at the departing figures. They were lost for words. They were lost for ideas, too. Warren took a look at his brother, who just looked stunned. No one smaller or younger than any of his teachers had ever spoken to him like that before. There was only one thing to do. Craig swung round and hurled the lamb into the pond. Then he and his brother fled.

As they came out from behind the hedge, Nathan spotted Alex and Tim. "Gosh," he said suddenly. "Look over there, George!" He pointed at nothing across the playground, and as George looked, he whispered to Tim: "It's over to you," and disappeared into Tim's pocket.

"Thanks a bunch," Tim said, as George turned back to his saviour. On seeing Tim, he blinked.

"How did you do that?" he asked in amazement.

"What?" asked Tim.

"Change back into you school clothes? You were in your shepherd clothes: now you aren't any more."

"You were seeing things," said Tim weakly.

"Didn't you know Tim wants to be a magic man when he grows up?" put in Alex. "Anyway, we'd better do something about you. You are, if you don't mind my saying so, the most disgusting mess I've ever seen."

"My lamb," George wailed, as Alex began marching him towards the cloakroom.

"Tim will rescue him, won't you, Bunnikins?" said Alex with a grin.

Tim winced. Carefully, he looked around for any sign of

44

a teacher before cautiously crawling through the hedge. Edging forward, he tried to reach the sodden lamb. He was reluctant to try paddling in the icy water. There seemed nothing for it but to pick a branch of the hedge and use this to pull the toy towards him, together with half the pond's growth of algae. At last, he stood up, triumphant, holding aloft one very wet lamb, from which hung slimy green bits of every description. Swinging round, he almost hit a brick wall, clad in a maroon puffer jacket.

"So, Timothy Stephens, this is how you spend your break, is it?" said the wall.

"Uh, sorry, Mrs. Hodge," mumbled Tim.

"I really don't know what to do with you any more," said his teacher, folding her arms across her wide chest. "You really have been behaving very oddly these last two days."

"I… I didn't mean it."

"No doubt. No one ever does – unless his name is Ches– never mind. You know you've broken one of the school's most important rules, don't you? What is it?"

"Never to go to the nature area without an adult," Tim muttered. The lamb was still in his hand, and was dripping on to Mrs. Hodges' lace-ups.

"So – what have you to say? Why were you here?"

"I had to rescue this for George." said Tim.

"And how did it get into the pond?"

Tim longed to tell his teacher, but he knew the consequences of ratting on a Chesney.

So he hung his head instead. "It sort of flew," said Tim.

"Flew? From where did it sort of fly?"

"From over there." Tim pointed towards where the two sweatshirts were still playing 'goal posts'.

"So, what were you doing? Playing football with little George's lamb? Tim, I'm truly disappointed in you."

Tim hung his head. "Yes, Mrs. Hodge – sorry, Mrs. Hodge," he heard himself say. What rubbish he was speaking at that moment, he thought. He sounded like one of the Chesneys when they got caught with their hands on someone else's packed lunch!

"Well, this isn't the best time to send you to Mrs Adams," said Mrs Hodge, "with the play about to start. And, as this is the first time I've ever caught you doing something like this, I'll let it go for the moment. Just be sure it doesn't happen again! Now, you'd better see if you can rinse that mess out."

"Thank you, Mrs. Hodge," Tim murmured.

In the cloakroom, Alex had just finished wiping and drying George's face for a second time. The infant crowed with delight when he saw his pet, despite its bedraggled appearance. Tim filled a wash-basin with warm water and plunged the toy into it. The water immediately turned greeny-brown.

"It's about time the pond was cleaned out," said Alex, turning his head away from the stink which arose from the wash-basin. He glanced at Tim, who was staring wide-eyed into space. "What's your problem?" Alex asked.

"What? Oh… I…" Tim's refocused his eyes. "Sorry… I… well, I got caught."

"What?" exclaimed Alex. Who by? Stodge?"

"'Fraid so," muttered Tim.

"That's bad."

"I'll live," said Tim with a sigh. "Let's get George's lamb rinsed out first. Here–" He handed the soggy, mud-coloured lump of wool to its small owner, who stared at it sorrowfully.

"Put it on the radiator in Miss Rennie's classroom," said Alex. "It'll look better when it's dry." Cuddling the toy to his chest so that a brownish damp mark started to spread across his shirt front, George set off for the Infants' classroom.

"Well, what do you think about my double?" Tim asked Alex. "Taking on the Chesneys like that – how did he do it, I wonder?"

"Why should a couple of big bullies worry me?" said a voice. Nathan was out of Tim's pocket once more. "I've had to scare off wolves, remember? Those boys were nothing – they're frightened of their own shadows."

"But if any of us tells them to do something, they try to take our heads off," said Tim. "You told them to give the lamb back and they just stood there."

"That's because I meant it," said Nathan. "They knew I wasn't scared of them. Now you're not to let me down," he said to Tim. "They think you were me out there – don't let them scare you ever again."

"I'll try," said Tim, feeling very scared indeed.

CHAPTER TEN

GO FOR IT!

Hardly anyone remembered what they had had for lunch that day. All the children had been just too excited about the play to concentrate on their food. Tim had finished his sandwiches in record time – or so it seemed. He had, in fact, eaten only the egg mayonnaise one – his favourite – and carried the cheese and tomato one, still in its clingfilm, to a corner of the playground, before releasing Nathan.

"Can you tell me what this is?" asked the shepherd boy, sniffing it cautiously.

"Food," said Tim. "Just eat it. You need to keep your strength up. And when you've finished, we'd better go back into school. They'll be changing for the play in about ten minutes."

"Tim! Tim!" George came stumbling across the playground holding out his lamb. Its fleece was not quite the gleaming white of the day before, but at least it had fluffed up a bit.

"Quick!" Tim whispered. "Into my pocket!" Stuffing the last of the bread into his mouth, Nathan obeyed.

"He's better," George lisped. "You maked him better."

"That's good," said Tim kindly, trying to sound more like Nathan. "Is he nearly dry?"

"Nearly," said George happily. An awkward silence followed, during which the small boy stepped from one foot to the other in a kind of dance. Tim was about to ask him if he wanted to go to the toilet, when George suddenly spoke up again. "Do you want to come to my house for tea?" he asked.

Tim opened his mouth and shut it again. Thanks a bunch, Nathan, he thought evilly. Now you've really dropped me in it. Tea with one of Miss Rennie's infants – that'll do a huge amount for my street-cred.

"Uh… I dunno," he said weakly. "Not tonight. I've got…" He couldn't think what he had got, but there had to be something. Then inspiration struck.

"You'll have to ask your Mum and Dad – and I'll have to ask mine – then we'll see. Now, we'd better go in. It's nearly time to change."

"Tim, can you help me, again?" Alex was struggling with his striped bathrobe. The classroom was even more chaotic than the day before – if that was possible. Mrs. Hodge was squeezing herself between desks completely hidden by school skirts, shirts, jumpers, socks and tights. She kept a keen eye on what was going on, however, tugging at an angel dress here and straightening wings or a halo there.

"I'll see to Alex," she said to Tim. "It's high time you began undressing, young man."

Tim had to go through the motions, he realised, even if he wasn't going to go on stage.

Carefully, he took the Christmas card out of his pocket and stood it on the desk. Then he removed his jumper and shirt. He was rummaging in his supermarket bag, tugging out the dressing-gown and tea-towel, when Mrs. Hodge spotted David struggling with his costume. It was what Tim had been hoping for. "I'm going to pretend to go to the cloakroom," he whispered to the boy in the Christmas card. "I'm taking you with me, and I'll hide. Then you can go back into the classroom and pretend to be me! Sorted!" To his teacher, he said, "Mrs. Hodge, please may I be excused?"

49

"Yes, all right, Tim, but please hurry!" came the frantic reply.

Heart pounding, Tim left the room, clutching the card. When he reached the cloakroom, however, he stopped. There was someone else there already. He was sitting on one of the benches, clutching one bare foot and rocking back and forth.

"What's wrong, Vishnan?" Tim asked. The boy quickly brushed away a tear. "Hurt my foot," he panted. He was clearly in some pain.

Tim took a closer look. Three small bumps, like the points of a triangle: even on his brown foot the bruises were beginning to show.

"Did Craig do that?" he asked. The other boy nodded.

"He wanted my crisps," he said. "If he'd asked, I'd have just handed them over. They were stale anyway – I'd nicked them from some stuff in my Dad's shop, which was past its sell-by date. He didn't have to trample on me. Did you know those boots have metal studs? They're not allowed."

"Yeah, I know. I found out the same way as you did," said Tim. "So, who's going to tell Mrs. Adams, then?"

"Not me, that's for sure," said Vishnan. "I want to stay alive a bit longer."

"Me, too," said Tim. He wriggled as he felt something move in his pocket, and he brightened.

"Actually," he said, "there may be a way of sorting Craig out, without actually telling tales. I'll keep you posted."

"Thanks," said Vishnan. The pain in his foot seemed to be subsiding. "I'd better go and get changed. It takes a million hours to get into my costume with all that padding." He stood up and hobbled out of the cloakroom.

"Right," said Tim, "time for the Big Swap – before anyone else comes in!" A few moments later, Nathan was heading back to the classroom. "Phew!" said Tim as he locked himself in one of the cubicles. He intended to stay there until he heard the choir start singing the first carol.

"Tim! TIM! Where are you?" It was Alex's voice. "Mrs. Hodge is going frantic. Tim!" There came knocking on the door. "Are you sick or something?"

Reluctantly, Tim unlocked the door. "I'm not going on," he whispered.

"Not going on where?" said Alex, looking shocked. "On stage? But… you have to!"

"Shh!" said Tim. "I've set it up so that Nathan goes on instead of me–"

"But Nathan's not doing it either."

"What do you mean? He went back into the classroom, pretending to be me!"

"Yeah, well," said Alex. "I think he's sort of changed his mind. Unless Warren or George carry him on as a Christmas card."

"WHAT?" yelled Tim. He hurtled out of the cubicle and back into the classroom. The Christmas card had mysteriously transported itself back on to Tim's desk. Not only was Nathan standing on his hilltop above Bethlehem, he was wearing a blue dressing-gown and Tim's mother's tea-towel as well! Tim threw himself on to his knees beside the card, with tears streaming down his face. "Nathan," he begged, "What are you doing? You're supposed to be out here, taking my part. Come on, Nathan, please."

Very faintly, Tim heard a voice, as if from a distant hilltop. "Go for it!" it said.

Tim stood up, just as Mrs. Hodge's huge frame filled the doorway. "Are you all right young man?" she said, not unkindly.

"Yeah," lied Tim, hastily wiping his nose.

51

Mrs. Hodge moved nearer and bent forward so that her face was close to Tim's ear. "You're not upset about being caught in the Nature area, are you?" she asked, very kindly. Tim, who thought having a telling-off from his teacher was the least of his worries right now, nodded, nevertheless.

"Well, it's OK," she said. "Miss Rennie got the true story out of George. So don't worry – you behaved very responsibly in the circumstances. And take your time about changing – you've got a few minutes yet." Signalling to Alex to follow, she left him alone.

Tim turned and glared at the boy on the Christmas card, wearing his dressing-gown. What was he going to do about a costume now? Then he glanced at the rough, woven garment spread out on the table in front of him, and the beautiful blue checked head-cloth, with its fringe of tassels, neatly folded on top.

"You mean me to wear these?" he asked the card. Nathan, in his funny make-shift shepherd's costume, grinned back. Cautiously, Tim began to pull the homespun garment over his head. It felt itchy against his skin. But suddenly he felt quite good – almost like a real shepherd. Then he positioned the head-cloth on his head, using its circlet of braid to keep it in place. He took a look at himself in the mirror which Mrs. Hodge had brought into to school specially, and was amazed at the figure which stared back at him. He could have been Nathan – a real shepherd boy! As he left the classroom, he turned and gave the Christmas card the thumbs-up. Nathan imitated the gesture back.

CHAPTER ELEVEN

THE SHEPHERD'S REVENGE

The choir had almost finished their first carol when Tim joined his fellow-actors in the wings. He dared one peek round the curtain and drew back sharply. The hall was full to bursting. There were parents, aunts, uncles and little brothers and sisters – not an empty chair anywhere. A few fathers were having to stand at the back.

The young performers sensed the atmosphere and responded. Everyone seemed to have gone up a gear in his or her acting – lines spoken clearly and crisply, and with real feeling. The choir had never sung so sweetly. Mrs. Adams was standing in the wings on the other side of the stage, looking more and more relieved as the play progressed.

Now it was the turn of the Three Wise Men to visit King Herod's palace in Jerusalem. They processed majestically down the central aisle and swept regally up on to the stage, their rich, red, green and blue cloaks adding a touch of dignity. Craig approached Herod seated on his throne, and spoke up.

"We seek the Child they call the–" Suddenly, he stopped and stared at something behind one of the courtiers. He tried again. "We seek the King they call the Kong of Kongs," he said. "The Child they King the Call of Kings – the King of Kongs." A titter arose from the audience; it developed into chuckles until everyone was laughing discreetly, but laughing nevertheless. Tim, who was waiting in position to climb on to the make-shift hillside at the back of the stage, tried to see what was distracting Craig, and had to stop himself from laughing out loud. Nathan was standing below the level of the stage, and just behind the throne. Only his top half was visible. In his hand was one of Craig's precious football boots and in the other, a tiny spanner – the sort used to tighten up the studs. Only this time, he was busily unscrewing them one by one and dropping them through a crack in the stage. Craig's face was turning an ever deeper shade of beetroot as, helpless, he watched this act of vandalism.

Suddenly, he could stand it no longer and launched himself at Nathan, scattering King Herod's courtiers to left and right. He slid full length across the stage on his belly, his outstretched hand clutching air where the shepherd-boy should have been. As he skidded to a stop, he came nose to toe with his football boot, lying wonkily on its two remaining studs. Of the pesky boy in the blue dressing-gown, there was no sign. A piece of paper – or it might have been a Christmas card – fluttered to the floor behind the stage.

Gathering himself up on to his knees, Craig let out an almighty wail. Then he scrambled to his feet, turned and ran back down the steps and up the aisle, his cloak flying out behind him like Batman's, with Mrs Adams charging after him.

It was left to Mrs Hodge to try to restore order on stage. "Lewis!" she shouted above the general racket, "Your line please." Lewis needed prompting, but, to the sounds of "Shush!" all round the hall, the play proceeded once more.

Tim slipped from his place beside the other waiting shepherds, retrieved the Christmas card and went crawling behind the piled-up benches which formed the hill at the back of the stage. The figure on the card was sitting hugging his knees and giggling silently.

"You're making it worse for me," whispered Tim. "Craig

won't be satisfied, now, until I'm dead."

"Don't you believe it," said Nathan, suddenly growing to human size. "He's really been shown up for the big baby he is. Anyway, he's got another line to say later on, when he brings his gift to the Christ Child. I'm not planning to make a fool of him a second time."

"You really messed up the play, you know that, don't you?" said Tim.

"I don't know about that," came the cheerful reply. "Say I livened things up a bit. It was beginning to get boring."

"Tim!" came Warren's voice. "Where are you?"

Tim re-joined the other shepherds just in time to clamber up on to their hill. As they pretended to fall asleep, George suddenly did a very strange thing. "Do you want to give my lamb to the Baby Jesus?" he whispered shyly to Warren. The Big Shepherd stared at the tiny boy.

"Nah – it's yours," he whispered back, when he'd gathered his jaw back off the floor.

After Gabriel's speech, and as the trio were circling the hall on their journey to Bethlehem, George said again, "You can if you like."

"I know," whispered Tim, "Warren, you carry it until you get to the crib, then pass it to George to give to the Baby Jesus."

This time, Warren managed to ring the Inn bell without pulling the whole makeshift wall down. He spoke his line like a professional. Tim followed, his words ringing through the hall loud and clear. Then came George's line. At the mention of a 'lickle lamb', Tim held his breath. Was Warren going to hand the toy over or not? With a sudden gesture, the Biggest Shepherd passed it over to George and a sympathetic "Aah" spread through the audience.

The trio followed the Innkeeper to the part of the stage

where Mary and Joseph were waiting, and approached the crib, now much more stable thanks to some emergency carpentry work performed on it the afternoon before. As George presented his offering, Tim looked into the straw and for a brief moment he could have sworn he saw the Baby's eyelids flutter and the mouth curve into a smile. There was a faint glow surrounding the crib which no electric lighting could have produced. All three shepherds seemed to sense the atmosphere as they reverently knelt down.

To the singing of 'We Three Kings of Orient Are', Craig, Lewis and Christian now processed down the aisle. Mrs. Adams had managed to convince Craig that it was quite safe for him to go on stage to present the Baby Jesus with his casket of gold without fear of being laughed at a second time. She had also warned him that she would be confiscating the football boots as soon as the play was over.

"I bring you gold, for a King," Craig announced in a voice that resonated round the hall.

"Frankincense is my gift to the Son of God," said Lewis.

"And myrrh for suffering and death," said Christian. Once they had placed their gifts in the crib, they, too, knelt down. Thus, with shepherds on one side and Kings on the other, the Holy Family in the centre, Angel Gabriel looking down from her ladder half-hidden by some fluffy stuff trying to be a cloud, and the Star swinging gently above, the pageant of the Nativity was complete.

With the audience joining the choir and cast in a rendering of 'Oh Come All Ye Faithful' which threatened to blast the roof off the school, the performance ended to enthusiastic applause.

CHAPTER TWELVE

THE ICING ON THE CAKE

"Well, thank goodness that's over for another year," said Mrs. Adams, as she sipped a welcome cup of tea. She took a mince pie from the plate which Sima, still wearing her Virgin Mary costume, had shyly offered her.

"It was a great success," said Tim's mother. "I don't know how you manage with such a big cast."

"Well, it didn't all go smoothly," said Mrs Adams, thinking with a shudder of the boot episode, "but, anyway, you must be very proud of your Tim. He was so good, I think I'll give him a bigger part next year, when he's in Year Five."

"I'm sure he'll be thrilled," murmured his mother, not at all convinced.

In the classroom, with everyone grabbing at bits of school uniform, not paying much attention to whether they belonged to themselves or someone else, Tim and Alex grinned at one another. "You did it!" said Alex. "You thought you couldn't but you have."

Tim glanced at the Christmas card and winked at the tiny figure there, now wearing his own tunic once more. "Yeah," he said modestly. "It wasn't all that bad in the end."

"Let's go and get a cake," said Alex, pulling his sweatshirt carelessly over his head and stuffing his arms into the sleeves.

"I'll join you in a minute," said Tim. "I've got something important to say to a certain person – you know." Alex nodded sagely.

Tim picked up the card and headed towards the cloakroom. Once there, he placed it carefully on one of the benches and knelt down beside it.

"I know you've tried to help me," he began. "You were right to make me do my part in the play, and that stuff with Craig and George – well, you tried to make it better, anyway. I'm not sure it'll work."

"Trust me," answered Nathan, suddenly full-sized and sitting on the bench among the anoraks and coats. "It will. Just have faith in yourself, like when you were in the play."

"Yes… OK," said Tim. "But can you do me one very big favour? Don't try anything with my sister, thinking you'll get her to be nice to me. It won't work."

Nathan spread his hands out in front of him. "I'm only a little shepherd boy from Bethlehem," he said. "I can make some things happen, but miracles…" He shook his head. Both boys laughed.

"Thanks," breathed Tim with relief. "Shall I fetch you a cake? They're having tea and cakes in the hall."

"Honey cakes?" inquired Nathan, his eyes bright.

"I don't know about that. I'll get what I can."

As Tim wandered into the hall, he heard his name called. George was charging across to him, pulling two grown-ups behind him like harnessed cattle. "Tim!" he shouted. "Mummy, this is Tim. Can he come to tea – pleeze?"

"Not tonight, darling," said the pretty young woman whose hand George was clutching. "We're going to visit Uncle Cedric and Aunt Lavinia tonight. What about tomorrow?"

"I'll have to ask my Mum," mumbled Tim, unable to think quickly enough for an excuse. "Thanks," he added as an afterthought.

"Where is your mother?" Mrs. Wilkie asked. "I'd better

discuss arrangements with her."

This is going to be all round the school in a flash, thought Tim, as he led George and Mrs. Wilkie to where Mrs. Adams was still deep in conversation with his Mum. Once the introductions had been made, Mrs. Wilkie began at once to tell the others how kind Tim had been to her little George. Tim escaped to the serving hatch. All this praise being heaped on his head was beginning to unnerve him – especially as most of it was Nathan's doing.

"Would it be OK if I took two cakes, please, Mrs. Patel?" he addressed Sima's mother, who was in charge of the refreshments. "One for me and one for my friend who came to watch the play?"

"Go ahead," beamed Mrs Patel. She liked Tim, who was always polite when he came into the shop.

"Nearly as tasty as my mother's honey cakes," Nathan commented through a mouthful of crumbs. "What's the white stuff on top?"

"It's called icing," said Tim.

"Well, the crumbly bit is nice, but the i-cing makes it even better," said Nathan, licking the sugary paste off with his tongue.

"Precisely," said Tim. He suddenly felt rather tired. The day had gone well – much better than he could ever have dreamed. As a reward, he was to be a guest at the home of a baby in Miss Rennie's infant class. The icing on the cake it wasn't.

"Look, do you mind getting back into my pocket?" Tim asked his friend, as the last crumb disappeared. "Mum will be looking for me in a minute." Nathan cheerfully obliged and he and Tim emerged into a slowly emptying hall.

"Tim!" David drew level with him. "George hasn't really asked you to tea, has he?" he asked.

"What if he has?" growled Tim. "I don't have to go, do I?"

"I would," said the future rocket scientist. "My little sister, Sarah, went to his house – or should I say, farm – when it was his birthday. And do you know what he got for a present?" What he said next made Tim's eyes light up.

"You don't say," he breathed. "Would he let me have a go, do you think?"

"Hello," said a cheery voice, which Tim only half recognised. Sophie, holding Sima firmly by the wrist, had joined the pair. With a mumbled 'gotta go,' David escaped. He had chosen not to mess with Tim's big sister. "Who played the shepherd instead of you?" Sophie demanded. "He was much better than you." Tim felt himself turn scarlet.

"Only winding you up," Sophie said with a laugh. "You weren't bad – not bad at all." A compliment indeed. But his sister wasn't finished.

"And someone says you rescued George from the Chesneys – if you weren't my brother, I'd say I was almost proud of you!"

Tim gawped at his sister. Had something fallen on her head, he wondered – the Star, maybe? Was she sickening for something – or was she in love? Never in all his nine years had she ever said anything the least bit complimentary to him – yet she had just sung his praises, in her own weird sort of way, admittedly, twice in the space of a minute! Before he could find the words to respond, she went on, "Sima wants to say something." She thrust the smaller girl forward.

Sima looked up at him with dark, melting eyes. "Would you like to be my boy-friend?" she asked shyly. Tim gulped. Girls! Why did they always have to complicate things?

Something thumped him in the chest, and it wasn't the beating of his heart. Much as he longed to hear Nathan's opinions on this latest development, he had to resist. He would have to wait until bed time, when they were alone.

As he stepped outside the hall into the cold winter sunshine, three figures blocked his path. Their smirks were a warning of something unpleasant to come. But Tim had his secret weapon. He looked each boy in turn in the eye. Interesting, he thought: suddenly, I'm eye to eye with Warren. I'm nearly as big as he is.

"Who's your best mate then?" Craig began. "No – don't tell me…"

In a chorus, they chanted "Georgie Wilkie, Baby Georgie!" When Tim made no attempt to break through the ring, they tried again. "You going to his housey-wousey, then, Timmy-Wimmy?" Christian taunted him.

"You're catching on," said Tim, cheerfully. "Going to ride on his quad bike, actually – you knew he had one, did you?" As the group parted, he sauntered off to join Alex and his mother waiting by the gate. Glancing back, he saw them still standing where he had left them. They were rooted to the spot, three black holes where their mouths should be.

*

"Thanks, Nathan," said Tim to the smiling shepherd boy on the card, as he climbed into bed that night. "You did me a lot of favours today. I'm not sure about that last one – I don't think I'm quite ready for a girl-friend, yet!"

Stepping neatly off the card, Nathan put himself at the end of the bed. "You don't get it, do you?" he said.

Tim looked at his new friend, mystified. "What don't I get?"

"That girl – Sima, did you say she was called? She's the She-wolf's best friend – yes?" Tim nodded. "Would your sister let her best friend become your girlfriend if she still hated you? It's her way of showing that she's not embarrassed by you any more. You've won!"

"So I have," said Tim, staring at the design on his duvet cover. Finally he looked up.

"I hope you didn't find the play too stupid. I don't suppose it was anything like that when the real Baby Jesus was born."

"Know what I think?" said Nathan after a pause. "You say there are plays like this everyhere to celebrate the Messiah's birth?" Tim nodded. "Well, I think that whatever the play is like, stupid or not, so long at the people taking part try their best, the Messiah is there. Do you understand what I'm saying? Every time there is a – what did you call it? A Nativity Play – the Birth of the Messiah takes place again. He becomes a Baby again and lies in the manger. You felt His presence – you all did."

"But that was Jessica – Emma's doll," said Tim.

"Pull the other one," said Nathan with a grin. He stood up. "Time I went home. My father and brother will be going crazy, wondering where I've got to."

"I hope you won't get into trouble," said Tim. "Will you visit me again some time?"

Nathan looked thoughtful. "I'll never forget this day – or you, and your crazy sister. It's been great, but – well – maybe I should stay in my own time from now on. You never know when something might go wrong – and I really would miss my hills and valleys around Bethlehem."

"Maybe you're right," Tim murmured. Sadly, he watched his friend move back towards the card, take up his position, and wave, before freezing there. "Still forgot his tea-towel," he thought drowsily as he pulled the duvet up round his neck.

*

"What's that you're clutching?" said a voice in his ear. Tim rolled over sleepily.

"What?" he said. Was it morning already?

"It's that strange head-cloth you were wearing in the play," said Tim's mother, opening his curtains. A single star winked at him through the window.

"Oh, yes," said Tim, sitting suddenly upright. "Nathan–"

"Was he the boy who lent it to you?" his mother asked, absent-mindedly straightening the duvet. "You ought to try to get it back to him."

"Yes, only…" Tim glanced at the card. Hillside and town alike were bathed in sunshine. Of Nathan there was no sign.

"Only what?" asked his mother.

"Only, I think he's left the country," said Tim.

"Permanently, you mean? He'll be back some time, surely."

Tim tightened his grip on the cloth. "I'll keep it safe," he said, "just in case."

THE END

About the Author

Monica Withrington was born and educated in South Africa.

Although trained as a teacher, she has told and written stories all her life, some of which have been published.

She now lives with her English husband in the Midlands, where she enjoys the inspiration she receives from her three young granddaughters.

'The Reluctant Shepherd' is her first novel for children.

Note from the Author

Thank you for reading 'The Reluctant Shepherd'. I hope you enjoyed it and would be very grateful if you would leave a review. Thank you.

If you would like to know more about my writing, I would love to hear from you. My email address is mwithrington@googlemail.com.

Printed in Great Britain
by Amazon